The Monster Cake-eater

Published in the UK by Scholastic Education, 2022
Scholastic Distribution Centre, Bosworth Avenue, Tournament Fields, Warwick, CV34 6UQ
Scholastic Ireland, 89E Lagan Road, Dublin Industrial Estate, Glasnevin, Dublin, D11 HP5F

SCHOLASTIC and associated logos are trademarks and/or registered trademarks of Scholastic Inc.
www.scholastic.co.uk
© 2022 Scholastic
1 2 3 4 5 6 7 8 9   2 3 4 5 6 7 8 9 0 1

Printed by Ashford Colour Press
The book is made of materials from well-managed, FSC®-certified forests and other controlled sources.

A CIP catalogue record for this book is available from the British Library.

ISBN 978-0702-30917-5

All rights reserved. This book is sold subject to the condition that it shall not, by way of trade or otherwise, be lent, hired out or otherwise circulated in any form of binding or cover other than that in which it is published. No part of this publication may be reproduced, stored in a retrieval system, or transmitted in any form or by any other means (electronic, mechanical, photocopying, recording or otherwise) without prior written permission of Scholastic Limited.

Every effort has been made to trace copyright holders for the works reproduced in this publication, and the publishers apologise for any inadvertent omissions.

Author
Ann Hill
Editorial team
Rachel Morgan, Vicki Yates, Fiona Undrill, Liz Evans
Design team
Dipa Mistry, Justin Hoffmann, Andrea Lewis, We Are Grace
Illustrations
Letizia Rizzo/Astound

Help your child to read!

This book practises these letters and letter sounds.
Point and say the sounds with your child:

- o (as in 'no')
- a (as in 'waving')
- e (as in 'she')
- a-e (as in 'cake')
- i-e (as in 'mine')
- o-e (as in 'strode')
- u-e (as in 'duke')
- e-e (as in 'athlete')
- ew (as in 'news')
- ie (as in 'field')

Your child may need help to read these common tricky words:

the, of, to, oh, all, said, they, are, were, you, into, was, your, people

Before reading
- Look at the cover picture and read the title together. Read the back cover blurb to your child.
- Ask your child: *Have you read a story about a monster before? What did it do?*

During reading
- If your child gets stuck on a word, remind them to sound it out and then blend the sounds to read the word: th-r-ew, threw.
- If they are still stuck, show them how to read the word.
- Enjoy looking at the pictures together. Pause to talk about the story.

After reading
- Ask your child: *Do you think the monster will come back? Why not?*
- *How do you think people feel about the monster at the end of the story?*

The cake-eating monster strode out of her cave. She came across the fields to the town gates.
"Oh no!" shrieked the cake seller.

Each week, the monster came and ate *all* the cakes.

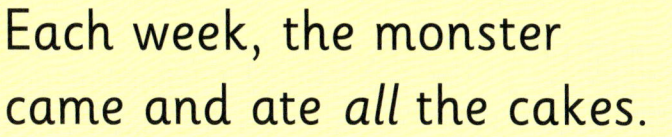

"I hope the monster won't eat these cakes!" said the baker, waving his rolling pin. "They are for the duke's wedding!"

"Those are mine...

...and these are mine!" yelled the monster.

Stop thief!

"Those were mine! Go home!" said the duke, shaking with fear.
"You are a rude and selfish beast!"

...and stomped back to her cave with a plate of cakes.

The duke crawled out, shaking with anger.

The next week, Pete gazed at the monster striding to town.

Pete was brave.

As the monster chewed, Pete back-flipped into the air.
He threw his rope and drew it tight.

Pete drove the sobbing monster home.

The crowd clapped.
"These are for you, Pete!" said the duke.

"Make your own cakes!" said Pete.
He threw a cookbook and apron down.

The monster baked a field of cakes and never came to town again. People even went to her for cakes!

Retell the story